Dancing
No Matter What

by Nomi J. Waldman
illustrated by Larry Johnson

 Harcourt

Orlando   Boston   Dallas   Chicago   San Diego

Visit *The Learning Site!*

www.harcourtschool.com

"Mother!"

As soon as she heard that, Mrs. Estrada knew something was wrong. She was usually "Mama" to all three of her girls, and it was only when there was a problem that she suddenly became "Mother."

She put down the dance costume she was mending to look up at her oldest daughter. Isabelle was standing in front of her, hands on hips, and her face was a storm about to burst.

"What is it, dear?" Mrs. Estrada asked, though she guessed that it had to do with the little sister who stood scowling in the doorway to the living room.

Isabelle pointed at Fortunata and began to sputter. "Do you know...do you know what she said to me? Do you know?"

Of course she didn't know, so she just waited for Isabelle to get it out. As she waited, she glanced from one girl to the other. Twelve-year-old Isabelle, her long, straight dark hair pulled into a knot behind her head, stood about two feet away, her slim dancer's body tight with anger. Right behind her now was the eight-year-old.

Except for having her long hair in braids, Fortunata was a smaller copy of her sister. How alike they are, thought their mother, yet they were always quarreling.

3

"She told me she hopes I break my leg!" Isabelle cried.

"Isabelle," her mother answered, puzzled, "you know that saying 'Break a leg' is just the way dancers and actors wish each other good luck. It isn't ever meant to be taken seriously."

"That's not what she said!" insisted Isabelle. "She said, 'I hope you break your leg,' and that's what she meant!"

Mrs. Estrada looked at Fortunata, whose scowl had grown even darker. "Yes, I admit it. I did say that. She was being so mean to me, talking all the time about how she was going to dance this, solo in that, and just be the greatest thing on toes there ever was."

"You're just jealous," snapped Isabelle, "because you can't dance with your thumpy old foot!"

As soon as she said it, she was sorry. She watched as her sister's eyes filled with tears. Fortunata turned silently and walked out of the room, the sound of her cast bumping on the floor.

"I...I'm sorry, Mama. I shouldn't have said anything about her cast." Isabelle spoke in a tone of voice very different from the one she had been using before.

Her mother shook her head. "I'm not the one you owe an apology to, Isabelle. It's already been a couple of months since Fortunata's operation, and she still has to wear a cast for another four weeks. It's hard for a little girl who loves to dance not to be able to. You should understand that more than anyone else does."

"I know, I know," said Isabelle, dropping down on the sofa next to her mother. "Still, it's not my fault, and she'll be able to dance again when the cast comes off. Dr. Martinez said she'd be even better because her foot would be stronger."

Mrs. Estrada didn't say anything but merely raised her eyebrows in a silent question.

"OK, you're right," Isabelle said quietly. "When you want to dance, three months is a long time." Suddenly she jumped up, shouting, "Time! Mama, it's almost five o'clock! I've got to get to warm-ups, and I still haven't packed my stuff!"

For the next ten minutes, there was much rushing around as Mrs. Estrada helped Isabelle fold and pack everything she would need for the warm-up and the performance.

Five-year-old Anna scampered in and out of the way, avoiding a collision with the flexibility of yet another future ballerina. Despite all the commotion, though, Fortunata never came out of her room.

Finally everything was ready, and with no time to spare. The Espositos pulled up right on time, and Isabelle squeezed into the van, already loaded with dancers, costumes, and bags of snacks. Isabelle waved to her mother as the van pulled away.

Mrs. Estrada knocked on Fortunata's bedroom door and walked in, with Anna following her. Seeing the look on her sister's face, though, Anna suddenly felt too timid to enter all the way and instead stood watching by the door.

Fortunata was scrunched up on her bed, trying to ignore both of them. Her mother gently removed the earphones from Fortunata's head and began to smooth the girl's dark braids.

"It isn't fair, Mama," Fortunata said finally.

"No, sweetie," her mother answered, "it isn't."

"I'm a good dancer, too. At least, I was."

"Yes, and you will be again," her mother responded.

"Maybe."

Mrs. Estrada stopped stroking her daughter's hair. "Maybe?"

"OK," said Fortunata, finally smiling, "I will be."

"That's better, because you know how important attitude is when you want to accomplish something. As Papa and I always say: If you're going to devote your time to something that means a lot to you, you have to believe you can do it."

"I do, and I will." Heartened by the smile on her sister's face, Anna crept onto the bed and rested her head on her older sister's shoulder.

Mrs. Estrada rose. "Good. Now, let's all get dressed. Papa will be home soon, and we'll have just enough time to eat before we go."

Fortunata shook her head. "I'm not going to that stupid recital," she said.

Her mother sighed. "We are all going, as a family. I can't very well leave you home alone. Besides, no matter how you feel, this is very important to Isabelle. Papa's making a videotape of her performance, and Isabelle is going to use it to apply for a scholarship to the School of the Arts. As much as Isabelle—and you—have thrived under the Andersons' teaching, it's time for her to move on to more advanced training."

This time it was Fortunata who sighed. "All right. I'll go, but I won't enjoy myself!"

Mrs. Estrada just smiled and nodded.

By a quarter to seven, the lobby outside the school auditorium was bustling with people. As they waited for Mr. Estrada to park the car and rejoin them, Mrs. Estrada saw many people she knew in the crowd. She recognized many of them as parents of the girls and boys who took classes at the Anderson Dance Studio with her daughters. All around her there were many cheerful greetings as friends shook hands or embraced each other.

Mrs. Estrada moved through the crowd so that she could congratulate Lydia Woo, who had just been accepted as an apprentice by an important dance company. "Your daughter Isabelle will be the next dancer to move up," said Lydia's mother as the two women embraced.

"We can only hope and try," said Mrs. Estrada, smiling at the thought. She reached down to take Anna's hand again and then looked for Fortunata. She finally spotted her other daughter leaning against a wall near the ticket-takers. Fortunata was staring off into space, clearly trying hard not to see or be seen by anyone. She appeared to be balancing herself on her good foot while trying to hide the one with the cast behind it.

Mrs. Estrada shook her head and wondered if there was anything she could do to make this evening come out right for Fortunata.

Just then the lobby lights blinked on and off, the signal for everyone to take their seats in the auditorium. Mr. Estrada rejoined the family and caught Fortunata's hand as he moved toward the doors.

Finally everyone was seated. The Estradas found four adjacent seats in the third row, but Anna ended up on her father's knee so that she could see better. As her parents looked through their programs, Anna proudly recited her sister's name each time she found it. Fortunata paid no attention, or at least she pretended that she didn't care.

The first four dances were quite varied, as each one was presented by a different class. First there was a ballet chorus by the youngest of the dance groups. Not all of the boys and girls were in step, but everyone seemed to be having fun, even the little girl who was still moving when the music stopped. The crowd applauded enthusiastically anyway.

Then came a more complex piece, with several soloists supported by small groups of dancers. Mrs. Estrada glanced over at Fortunata, because this had been her class. She was pleased to see that her daughter was caught up in the dance, moving her body ever so slightly with the music. Still, when the piece ended, Fortunata sat motionless and did not applaud.

The next level presented an original piece choreographed by Phil Esposito, Isabelle's friend. It related the story of a group of migrant workers, showing the hardships they had endured and finally overcome. It was very moving.

Just before the piece that would conclude the first part of the program, though, there was a longer-than-usual wait. Then Isabelle stepped out between the closed curtains.

"Ladies and gentlemen, girls and boys," she began, "the next piece is not on your program. It's called 'Dancing Sitting Down,' and it stars—you!"

There was a sudden buzz in the audience as people looked at each other in astonishment.

Isabelle continued. "Not everyone can dance like the girls and boys you've watched tonight, but everyone here can move with the music."

Now the audience was paying close attention. Isabelle went on to explain that she and Phil were going to show the audience a number of head, hand, and arm movements. "You will see that how dancers use their hands and arms and how they move their heads," continued Isabelle, "can be as important to the dance as how they move their feet."

With that, the curtain opened and Phil stepped out of the wings. He walked to the center of the stage, where a stool had been placed.

When he sat down, his back was to the audience. That way, as he demonstrated each gesture, he would be facing the same direction as everyone in the auditorium. Isabelle explained every movement as she taught it. Just about everyone in the audience took part, though some giggled as they did, and many were not nearly as graceful as Phil. Isabelle gave each movement a name. They were simple names that were easy to remember, like "looking into the distance," "waving good-bye," and "head bent in sorrow."

Finally, Isabelle said, "Now we're going to put these movements together to music to tell a story. I will call out the name of each movement, and Phil will demonstrate.

"'Dancing Sitting Down' tells the story of a young man on a train, setting out on a new adventure. He's waving good-bye to the family he loves. The dance is dedicated to my sister Fortunata, who can hardly keep from dancing, no matter what."

The music began. The audience danced, sitting down, no one more enthusiastically than the little girl in the third row. As the dance ended in a crash of piano chords, Phil swung around on the stool and seemed to take everyone into his outspread arms. The whole audience came to its feet.

Well, thought Mrs. Estrada, looking at her smiling, clapping daughters, I'd say this evening came out better than anyone could have expected.